PARASAUROLOPHUS

by Kathryn Clay

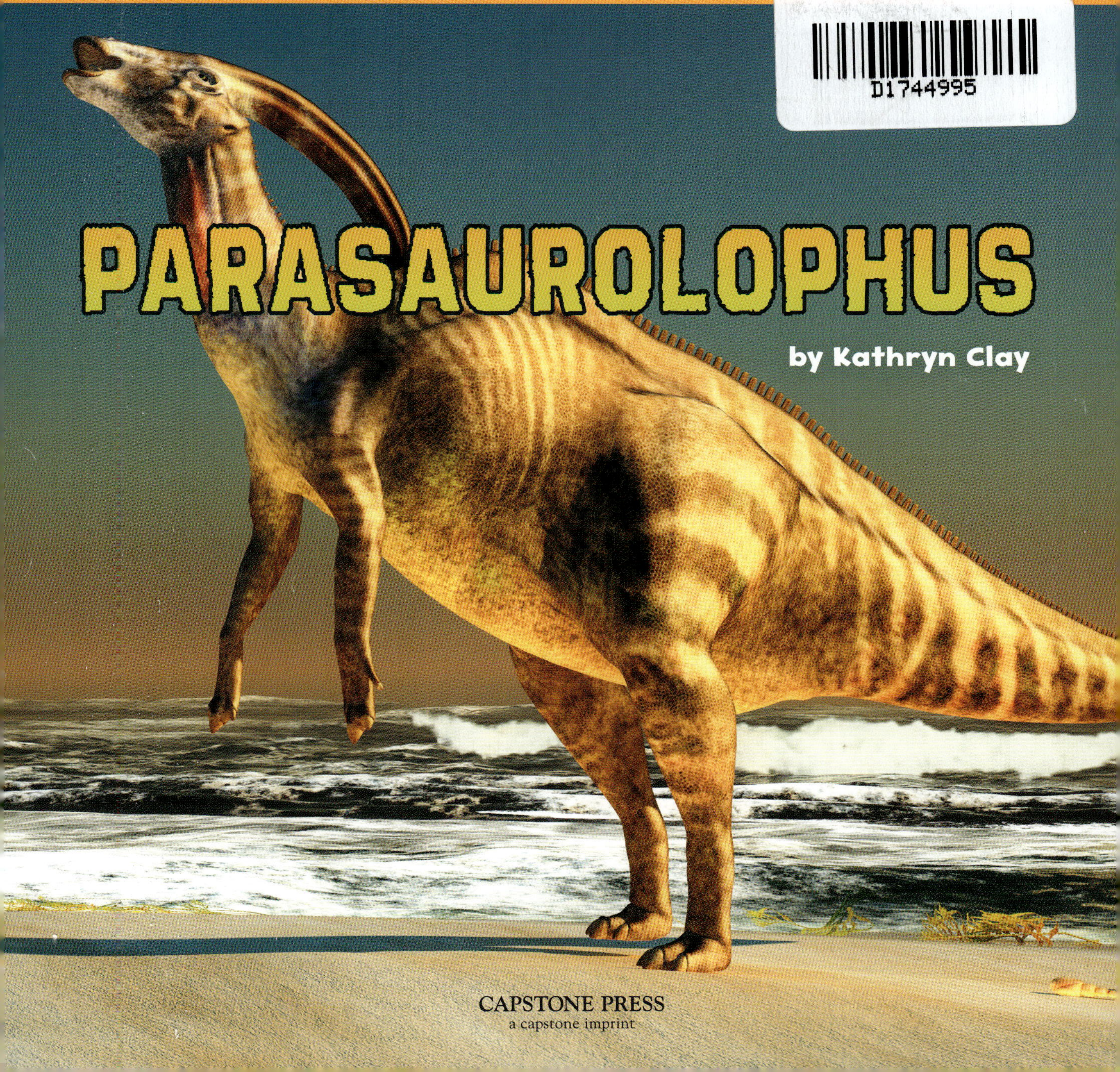

CAPSTONE PRESS
a capstone imprint

Little Explorer is published by Capstone Press,
1710 Roe Crest Drive, North Mankato, Minnesota 56003
www.mycapstone.com

Copyright © 2019 by Capstone Press, a Capstone imprint. All rights reserved. No part of this publication may be reproduced in whole or in part, or stored in a retrieval system, or transmitted in any form or by any means, electronic, mechanical, photocopying, recording, or otherwise, without written permission of the publisher.

The name of the Smithsonian Institution and the sunburst logo are registered trademarks of the Smithsonian Institution. For more information, please visit www.si.edu.

Library of Congress Cataloging-in-Publication Data

Library of Congress Cataloging-in-Publication data is available on the Library of Congress website.
ISBN 978-1-5435-5749-7 (library binding)
ISBN 978-1-5435-6013-8 (paperback)
ISBN 978-1-5435-5753-4 (eBook PDF)

Editorial Credits

Michelle Parkin, editor; Lori Bye, designer;
Kelly Garvin, media researcher;
Kathy McColley, production specialist

Our very special thanks to Matthew T. Miller, Museum Technician (Collections Volunteer Manager), Department of Paleobiology at the National Museum of Natural History, Smithsonian Institution, for his review. Capstone would also like to thank Kealy Gordon, Product Development Manager, and the following at Smithsonian Enterprises: Ellen Nanney, Licensing Manager; Brigid Ferraro, Vice President, Education and Consumer Products; and Carol LeBlanc, Senior Vice President, Education and Consumer Products.

Image Credits

Alamy/MasPix, 20-21, 30-31; Getty Images: John Cancalosi, 22, Kevin Schafer, 24; iStockphoto/rikkyal, 4, 15; Jon Hughes, cover, 2, 6-7, 9, 12-13, 16, 17, 23, 29 (b); Newscom/National News/ZUMA Press, 27; Science Source: Andrea Ferrari/NHPA/Photoshot, 5, Millard H. Sharp, 25 (t), Nobumichi Tamura/Stocktrek Images, 29 (t), Roman Garcia Mora/Stocktrek Images, 21; Shutterstock: Catmando, 1, 10, 18-19, catwalker, 25 (b), Daniel Eskridge, 14-15, Denis Vesely, 7, Elnarts, 28, topimages, 5 (b)

Printed and bound in the USA
PA48

TABLE OF CONTENTS

DINO FILE 4
DUCK-BILLED DINO 6
A PEEK AT THE BEAK 8
COMMUNICATING BY CREST 10
WEBBED WONDER 13
CRETACEOUS CREATURE 14
DANGER! 17
A DINOSAUR DINNER 19
TRAVELING TOGETHER 20
DINO YOUNG 22
FOSSIL FINDS 24
JOE THE PARASAUROLOPHUS 26
THE HADROSAUR GROUP 28

GLOSSARY 30
CRITICAL THINKING QUESTIONS 31
READ MORE 31
INTERNET SITES 31
INDEX 32

DINO FILE

name: Parasaurolophus

how to say it: pa-ra-sawr-OL-off-us

when it lived: Late Cretaceous Period, Mesozoic Era

what it ate: plants

size: 31 feet (9.4 meters) long
8 feet (2.4 m) tall
weighed 2.5 tons

Parasaurolophus was a dinosaur that stood out. The long, hollow crest on its head made Parasaurolophus easy to identify.

Parasaurolophus skull

Thanks to FOSSILS

A fossil is evidence of life from the past. Fossil bones, teeth, and tracks found in the earth have taught us everything we know about dinosaurs.

DUCK-BILLED DINO

Parasaurolophus belonged to a group of dinosaurs called hadrosaurs. These duck-billed dinosaurs had flat, bony beaks. Hadrosaurs had rows of teeth that could slice and grind up plants.

Other hadrosaurs include the large Shantungosaurus and small Probactrosaurus.

scaly skin

strong tail

long back legs

webbed feet

A Peek at the Beak

Parasaurolophus had a hard, toothless beak. It could rip through tough plants. Inside its cheeks, there were many layers of diamond-shaped teeth. The sharp teeth could easily chew up leaves from trees and bushes.

Parasaurolophus had hundreds of teeth. When a tooth wore down, another tooth grew in its place.

COMMUNICATING BY CREST

Parasaurolophus used the crest on its head to make noises and communicate with other Parasaurolophus.

Scientists wanted to know what Parasaurolophus's crest sounded like. Using powerful computers, the scientists scanned the dinosaur's skull. Then they made a 3D model. When air was blown into the crest model, it made a low, deep sound.

"The sound may have been somewhat birdlike, and it's probably not unreasonable to think they did songs of some sort to call one another."
—Carl Diegert, computer scientist

Scientists believe that Parasaurolophus's voice could be heard miles away.

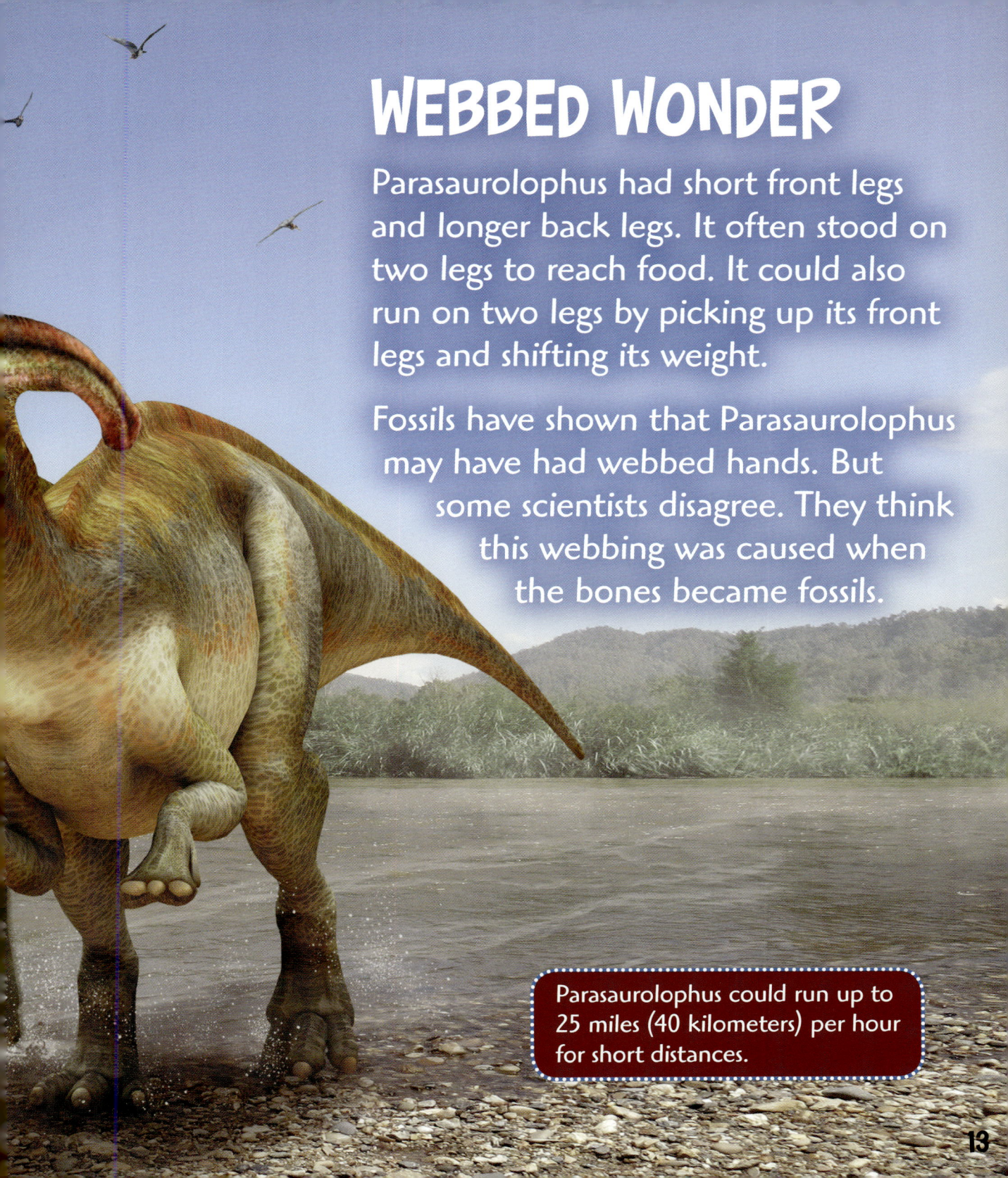

WEBBED WONDER

Parasaurolophus had short front legs and longer back legs. It often stood on two legs to reach food. It could also run on two legs by picking up its front legs and shifting its weight.

Fossils have shown that Parasaurolophus may have had webbed hands. But some scientists disagree. They think this webbing was caused when the bones became fossils.

Parasaurolophus could run up to 25 miles (40 kilometers) per hour for short distances.

CRETACEOUS CREATURE

The Cretaceous Period came after the Jurassic Period. During this time, the earth was warm and wet. Tropical plants covered the ground. Continents started separating from one another.

Parasaurolophus lived during this time. It roamed through forests and plains in what is now western Canada, Utah, and New Mexico.

OTHER CRETACEOUS ANIMALS

Tyrannosaurus Rex

Triceratops

Velociraptor

The Cretaceous Period lasted from 145 million to 66 million years ago.

DINOSAUR ERA

TRIASSIC — JURASSIC — CRETACEOUS

252　　200　　145　　66　　present

millions of years ago

DANGER!

Parasaurolophus had good eyesight. It could also hear well. The dinosaur could sense predators from a distance. Rather than fight a predator, Parasaurolophus often ran away before the danger got too close.

Parasaurolophus had to watch out for hungry meat eaters, such as Gorgosaurus and Albertosaurus.

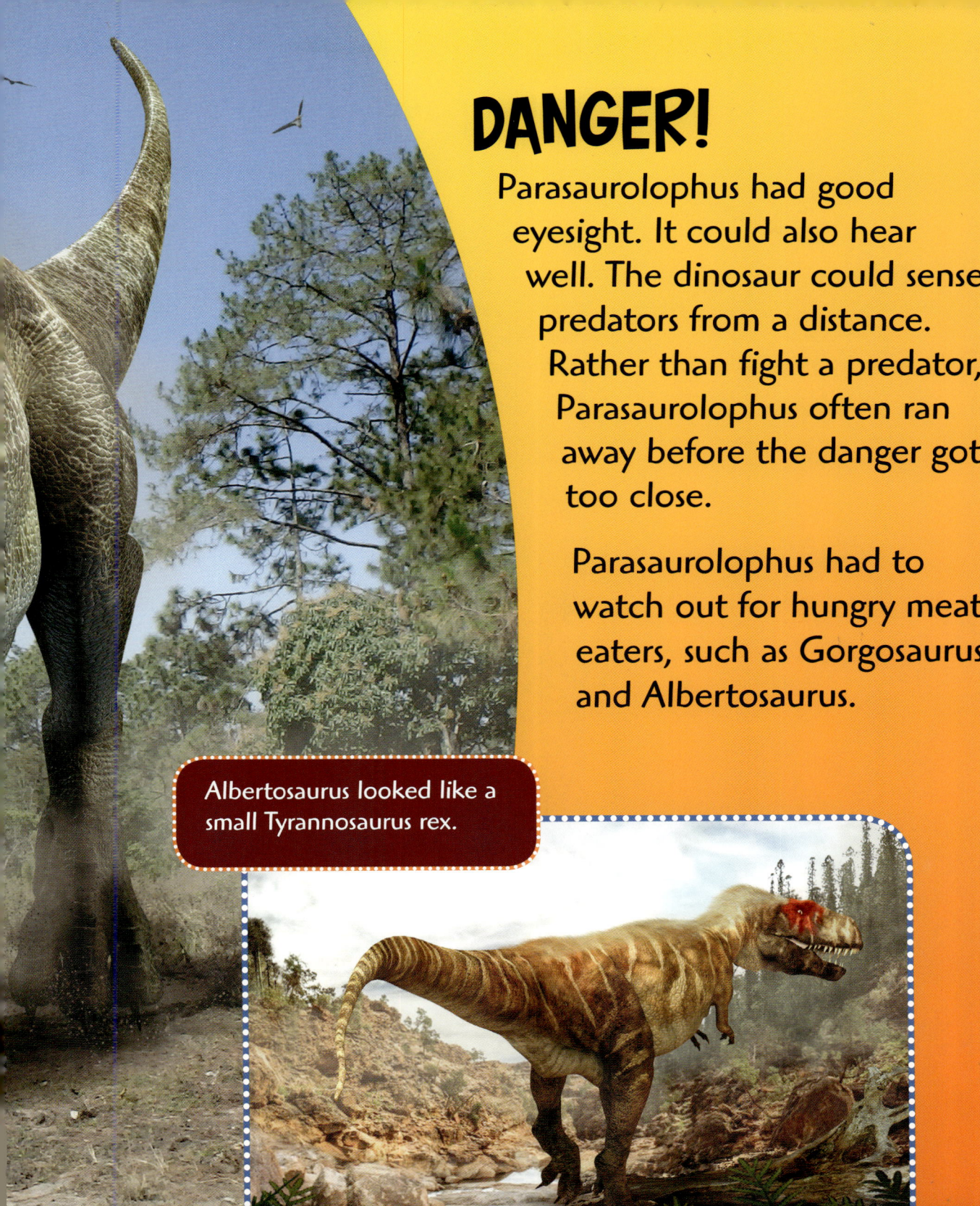

Albertosaurus looked like a small Tyrannosaurus rex.

Scientists can tell what Parasaurolophus ate by studying its fossils. They look at the dinosaur's teeth to see what types of plants they ate.

A DINOSAUR DINNER

Parasaurolophus was an herbivore. This means it ate only plants. Parasaurolophus ate ginkgo trees, pine needles, and leaves.

Most of the dinosaur's food came from plants on the ground. It also stood on its back legs to reach high leaves.

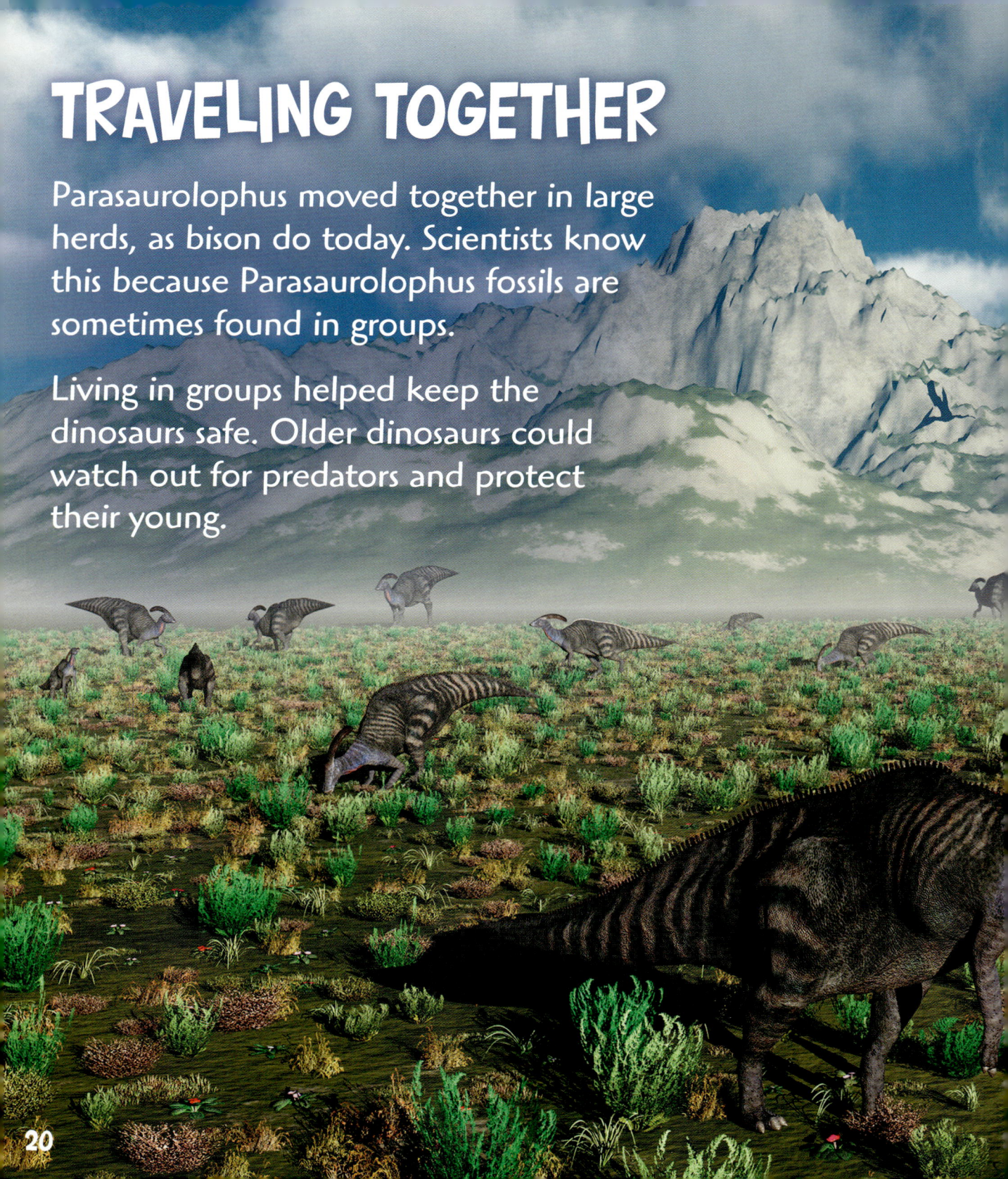

TRAVELING TOGETHER

Parasaurolophus moved together in large herds, as bison do today. Scientists know this because Parasaurolophus fossils are sometimes found in groups.

Living in groups helped keep the dinosaurs safe. Older dinosaurs could watch out for predators and protect their young.

Other hadrosaurs, such as Edmontosaurus, also traveled in large herds.

21

DINO YOUNG

Like most dinosaurs, Parasaurolophus laid eggs. They may have traveled to higher ground to build nests. This would have kept their eggs protected from flood waters.

Young Parasaurolophus had small crests by the time they were a year old. The smaller crests may have made high-pitched sounds that traveled short distances.

Dinosaur eggs have been found all over the world. But scientists often have to guess what type of dinosaur laid the eggs. The dinosaurs inside the eggs aren't usually fossilized. Scientists look for other fossils nearby to identify them.

FOSSIL FINDS

In 1920 paleontologist William A. Parks discovered the first Parasaurolophus fossil while digging in Alberta, Canada. It was a nearly complete skeleton. Two years later Parks named the dinosaur Parasaurolophus. It means *near-crested lizard*.

Parasaurolophus was featured on a U.S. stamp in 1997.

Today Parks's discovery is at the Royal Ontario Museum in Toronto, Canada. In 2007 an image of the skeleton was put on a $4 Canadian coin.

JOE THE PARASAUROLOPHUS

In 2009 the skeleton of a baby Parasaurolophus was discovered in southern Utah. High school student Kevin Terris found it during a school dig. He noticed a bone sticking out of a rock. It is the youngest and most complete Parasaurolophus skeleton ever found.

Terris named the skeleton "Joe." Today Joe's skeleton is at the Raymond Alf Museum in Claremont, California. Scientists at the museum digitally scanned Joe's bones. People can view the scans online.

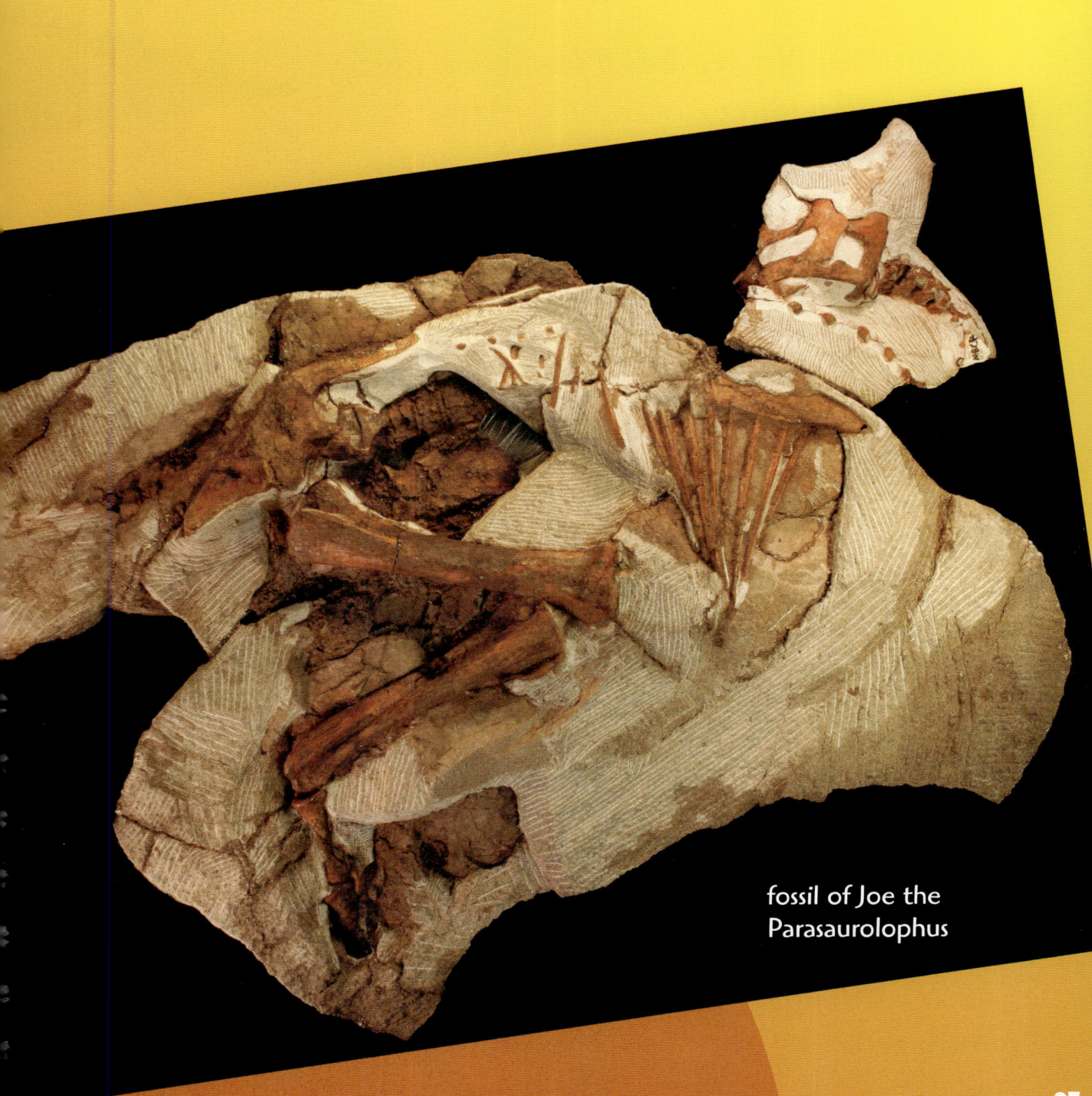

fossil of Joe the Parasaurolophus

THE HADROSAUR GROUP

Hadrosaur fossils have been found on every continent including Antarctica. Many different dinosaurs belonged in this group.

Corythosaurus (KOR-ith-oh-SAWR-us) was shorter than Parasaurolophus but weighed half a ton more. Its name means *helmet lizard*. Scientists thought its crest looked like the helmets worn by ancient Greek soldiers.

Charonosaurus (shar-OWN-oh-SAWR-us) fossils have been found in Asia. The dinosaur looked very similar to Parasaurolophus. But at 5.5 tons, Charonosaurus weighed much more.

Edmontosaurus (ed-MON-toe-SAWR-us) had a small, boneless crest. It was named after the Edmonton Formation, where the dinosaur's fossils were first discovered. Today this place is known as the Horseshoe Canyon Formation.

GLOSSARY

communicate (kuh-MYOO-nuh-kate)—to share information, thoughts, and feelings

continent (KAHN-tuh-nuhnt)—one of earth's seven large land masses

crest (KREST)—a comb or tuft of feathers, bone, or skin on the head of a bird or other animal

hadrosaurs (had-roh-SAWRZ)—a group of closely related dinosaurs with duck-billed snouts

herd (HERD)—a group of animals that lives or moves together

hollow (HOL-oh)—empty on the inside

identify (eye-DEN-tuh-fye)—to tell what something is

Mesozoic Era (mehz-uh-ZOH-ik IHR-uh)—the age of dinosaurs which includes the Triassic, Jurassic, and Cretaceous periods; when the first birds, mammals, and flowers appeared

paleontologist (pale-ee-uhn-TOL-uh-jist)—a scientist who studies fossils

plain (PLANE)—a large, flat area of land with few trees

predator (PRED-uh-tur)—an animal that hunts other animals for food

tropical (TRAH-pi-kuhl)—hot, wet, and humid

CRITICAL THINKING QUESTIONS

1. Parasaurolophus stood on its back legs to reach food. Name another plant-eating dinosaur that could stand on its back legs.

2. Why do scientists think Parasaurolophus traveled in herds? Name an animal today that travels in herds.

3. William A. Parks discovered Parasaurolophus in Alberta, Canada. List two other dinosaurs discovered in Alberta.

READ MORE

Rissman, Rebecca. *Edmontosaurus and Other Duck-billed Dinosaurs: The Need-to-Know Facts.* Dinosaur Fact Dig. North Mankato, MN: Capstone Press, 2017.

Sewell, Matt. *The Colorful World of Dinosaurs.* Hudson, NY: Princeton Architectural Press, 2018.

West, David. *Dinosaurs of the Cretaceous.* Prehistoric! Mankato, MN: Smart Apple Media, 2015.

INTERNET SITES

Use FactHound to find Internet sites related to this book.

Visit *www.facthound.com*

Just type in 9781543557497 and go.

Check out projects, games and lots more at *www.capstonekids.com*

INDEX

3D models, 11

Alberta, Canada, 24

beaks, 6, 7, 8

crests, 5, 6, 7, 10, 11, 22, 24, 28, 29
Cretaceous Period, 14–15

diet, 4, 8, 18, 19

eggs, 22
eyesight, 17

fossils, 5, 13, 18, 20, 22, 24, 28

hadrosaurs, 7, 21, 28–29
herds, 20, 21

Joe the Parasaurolophus, 26

legs, 6, 7, 13, 19

New Mexico, 15

Parks, William A., 24, 25
predators, 17, 20

range, 14
Raymond Alf Museum, 26
Royal Ontario Museum, 25

size, 4, 28, 29

teeth, 5, 8, 18
Terris, Kevin, 26

Utah, 15, 26